WRITTEN & ILLUSTRATED BY
CAROL DABNEY

"TWAS THE MOUSE BEFORE CHRISTMAS"

A CHRISTMAS TAIL

SPANISH INTERPRETATION BY
CINDY DABNEY REYES

EL RATONCITO Y LA NOCHEBUENA
UN CUENTO DE NAVIDAD

**Carol Dabney and Cindy Dabney Reyes are sisters
who live and work in Little Rock, Arkansas.**

Carol Dabney is the mother of five children and two grandchildren. At age sixteen she studied Italian Opera at the University of Arkansas in Fayetteville. She has written and illustrated several children's books: including "The Adventures of Noah" series, "Military Mommy," and her father's biography "Dance Me Home." Carol has been a radio disc jockey, music composer, choir director and resource teacher for twenty years.

Cindy Dabney Reyes is the mother of three children and four grandchildren. She graduated from Hendrix College majoring in Spanish and received her master's degree in education from the University of Central Arkansas in Conway, Arkansas. She has been a Spanish teacher for over twenty years in the Little Rock area.

Special Thanks to:
Barbara and John Funk, Phyllis Jones, Barry Tiemann, Mary and Richard Clark,
Ania Dabney, Jeff Woods, Robin Dabney, Kemper Funk, Sheri and Jay Park,
Charlie and Carol Johnson, Lucho Reyes, Mike Dabney, Christopher Lovins,
and Tamera Reyes..

This Christmas Story is Dedicated to:

The Children and Grandchildren of
Carol Dabney and Cindy Dabney Reyes:

Elena, Christopher, Gregory, John-Joseph,
Millie, Melissa, Michelle, Joshua-David.

Damien, Beth, Noah, Kiley, Dabney,
and Aliyah-Melelani.

This Book belongs

To:_____

Date:_____ From:

"Twas the Mouse Before Christmas"

You've heard it told about the night before Christmas, how everyone was asleep in the house: The children, the cat, and even the mouse.

But I say the truth is, there was one awake.

He was stirring up batter and baking a cake.

Has escuchado, "Era la Nochebuena y por toda la casa, no había ningún movimiento, ni siquiera un ratoncito.

Pero yo digo la verdad. Uno estaba despierto. Estaba batiendo para hacer un pastel.

He was in his corner of our little house,
there in the kitchen was Harold the mouse.

En un rincón de nuestra casita,
en la cocina, había un ratoncito, Harold.

Hark! Poor Harold could not fall asleep,

no matter how much he tried counting sheep.

He was so excited on this Christmas Eve about all the
things that Santa would leave.

Trató de contar ovejas, pero pobre
Harold no podía dormirse.

Estaba tan emocionado, pensando en las cosas que
iba a traer Santa esta Nochebuena.

So Harold stayed up to insure all went just right. The stockings were hung and the tree twinkled with light.

Así que Harold se quedó en pie para asegurar que todo estaba en su lugar, los calcetines colgados, y el árbol tiritaba con luces.

He set up the wiseman that the cat had knocked down,
while chasing her tail around and around.

Los Reyes Magos puestos, como el gato los había
botado, tratando de agarrar su propia cola.

Now all you could hear was the clock on the wall, and
Harold the mouse was having a ball.

Ahora, se escuchaba solo el reloj en la pared, mientras
Harold, el ratoncito, disfrutaba decorando la casa.

The cat was put out, and then brought back in.

Harold echó al gato, y después, lo entró.

The pups were asleep in their little pen.

Cada perrito se dormía en su camita.

He was humming a song he had just heard before,
when the carolers came to sing at the door. He felt
the magic of Christmas beginning to grow, when they
began singing and it started to snow.

El ratoncito pensaba en una canción que acababa
de escuchar cuando recién vinieron los cantantes
a la puerta.

Se sintió crecer la magia de la Navidad cuando
empezaron a cantar y comenzó a nevar.

So he put on his glasses and opened his book.

The one that says, "Best how to Cook."

Así que puso los lentes y abrió su libro nombrado,
"Mejor para Cocinar".

With his chef's hat nearby, he could not resist.

He said, "I'll give Santa cookies on my

best holiday dish."

Con su sombrero de cocinero puesto, no pudo resistir.

Dijo, "Yo le doy galletas a Santa, puestos en mi mejor

plato de Navidad."

He took out his bowl and his big wooden spoon,

flour and sugar in the full of the moon.

Sacó un contenido y su cucharón grande,

harina y azucar en la luz de la luna llena.

He put on his apron and stirred up his best,
then he tasted a little and baked up the rest.

Se puso su delantal y batió fuerte. Entonces,
probó un poco y cocinó el resto.

The smell of those cookies could be smelled around the world, while Santa was giving to each boy and each girl. Yes, Santa was busy, and Harold was too. Harold thought, "I'll serve milk with my cookies, that's just what I'll do."

Se sintió el olor de las galletas por todo el mundo, mientras Santa daba regalos a cada niño y niña.

Sí, Santa estaba ocupado y Harold también. El ratoncito pensó, "Yo voy a servir leche con las galletas." "Así va a ser."

Harold, the mouse was stirring alright.

He baked cookies for Santa all through the night.

Harold, el ratoncito, estaba en pie,

cocinando galletas toda la noche.

Then just before sunrise and all the baking
was done, poor Harold dosed off to sleep
and he missed all the fun.

Entonces, antes del amanecer, después de terminar
de cocinar, se durmió pobre Harold y perdió toda la
diversión que hubo después.

For the cat had new mittens.

El gato tenía guantes nuevos

Beamer the dog had a bone.

Beamer, el perrito tenía un hueso.

The children had shiny new toys all their own.

Los niños tenían sus propios juguetes,
brillantes y nuevos.

"Twas the Mouse Before Christmas"

The family gathered to give thanks for the day.

Entonces, la familia se juntó para dar gracias por el día.

But poor Harold was snoring,

I'm sorry to say.

Pero siento decir que pobre Harold roncaba.

Santa was so delighted by Harold's sweet gift. He left him a letter by the holiday dish.

A Santa, le encantó el dulce regalo de Harold. Así que lo dejó una tarjeta dando las gracias al lado del plato de Navidad.

Letter Santa wrote to Harold

Dear Harold,

I enjoyed the milk and cookies so much.

The reindeer love cake, so it was just the right touch.

On Christmas Eve, I want children to be asleep.

But since you're a mouse, I thought it was sweet.

I know you missed Christmas to bake just for me.

The joy of giving is worth it you'll see.

Cookies were what I needed to continue my mission.

So I hereby declare this a

"Mouse Before Christmas Tradition."

—SANTA

Merry Christmas!

THE END

La carta que Santa escribio a Harold

Querido Harold,

disfruté mucho de la leche y las galletas.

A los renos les encantaba el pastel. En la Nochebuena, quiero que se duerman los niños, pero, como tú eres un ratoncito, lo encontré tierno.

Ya sé que perdiste la Navidad cocinando para mí, pero la felicidad de regalar vale la pena, vas a ver.

Las galletas eran justo lo que yo necesitaba para continuar mi misión. Así que, por qué no llamamos a ésta,

una tradición del ratoncito y la Nochebuena?

Con cariño, SANTA

Feliz Navidad¡

FIN.

So when it is the night before Christmas and
your mom says, "Go to sleep."

Go straight to bed, and be sure not to peek!

Así que, cuando llega la Nochebuena y tu mamá te dice
que te duermas, anda derechito a la cama y no mires.

Harold's Famous Chocolate Chip Cookies

Pre-heat oven to 350 degrees

Ingredients:

1 cup real butter

1 cup white sugar

1 cup brown sugar

2 eggs

1 tablespoon real vanilla extract

Blend all these ingredients together in a large bowl.

In another bowl mix:

1 cup blended dry Quaker oatmeal

2 cups white flour

1 teaspoon baking soda

1 teaspoon cinnamon, 1 teaspoon nutmeg

1 teaspoon allspice, a pinch of salt

Stir altogether into wet ingredients along with

2 cups semisweet chocolate chips and 1 cup chopped walnuts

Bake for about 10 minutes. Taste and serve on your favorite holiday dish. Leave some out for Santa with milk on Christmas Eve.

Santa also likes other cookies and treats.

"Christmas in your Heart"
La Navidad esta en tu Corazon

Song Copyrights 1997.
Composed and recorded by Carol Dabney.
Spanish by Cindy Dabney Reyes.

"It doesn't have to snow for all of us to know

Don't need a Christmas tree for all of us to see

Christmas is like home with love so strong

No matter where you roam. To last your whole life long

It's not the tinsel, not the toys,

Not just for little girls and boys

Not just for the young you see,

but for anyone who can believe.

Christmas in your heart can last the whole year 'round

It doesn't have to wait till the frost is on the ground

From Manhattan's frosty snow…

to Hawaii's ocean mist

There's one thing I know you don't need…

mistletoe to kiss.

No importa adonde vas, ni donde estas.

La navidad esta en tu Corazon

Christmas is like home even when we're apart

No matter where you roam take Christmas

in your heart."

Christmas In Your Heart

Carol Dabney

Carol Dabney

"Christmas In your Heart"

Skye Ansara is a resident of Marked Tree, Arkansas. Skye is a singer musician who founded the band Opal Skye. www.wix.com/opalskye/home. Jennifer Ansara is originally from Maryland, and is a trained classical composer and award winning opera singer. Jen and Skye arranged the sheet music to "Christmas In Your Heart" to be included in the Carol Dabney's Christmas story "Twas The Mouse Before Christmas."

Carol Dabney composed and recorded "Christmas in your Heart" in the Hawaiian Islands on her "Picture of You" album in 1997, and again on her "When Miracles Come Our Way" album in 2003. The recording has the Spanish lyrics, interpreted by Cindy Dabney Reyes. Musical arrangement by Honolulu conductor Alwyn Erub at RKS Studios.

Picture of You musical album has the recorded version of *Christmas In Your Heart* plus the karaoke version for your little ones to sing too.

When Miracles Come Our Way all original gospel album sung by Carol Dabney and the Dabney family.

Music available at CDBaby. com

'Twas the Mouse Before Christmas children's book. https://www.amazon.com/author/dabneycdbooks. For a personally signed book from the author to your child/children order books online at Carol Dabney at ETSY. com Also available: Artwork prints from book and music. Plus Christmas story read on CD by the author. Music produced by Alwyn Erub.

caroldabney@wordpress.com

Other books and music by Carol Dabney is available. Contact for readings at carol.dabney@yahoo.com.

Dance Me Home military love story biography which is based on the true life story of Robert Jones Junior and his personal journey through WWII. Dance Me Home will find a place in your heart if you love American history and true romance.

Military Mommy is a children's picture poetry book of a military family, as seen through the eyes of five year old Noah. This charming story let's us appreciate our American Soldiers. www.amazon.com. Receive an autographed book by ordering Carol Dabney on Etsy.com

Merry Christmas

Reader Review 'Twas The Mouse Before Christmas children book

"Charming illustrations and the dedication of a little mouse named Harold make this story perfect. Grab your little ones and a plate of your own cookies (the recipe is in the back) and add this to your holiday traditions."~Mandi M. Lynch, author; owner of www.Inkmonkeymag. com Nashville, Tennesse

Carol is a very heartfelt writer, someone that writes from feel, and her works whether a song or a story, she's very insightful, Kudos to Carol! —Alwyn Erub, musical arranger, music minister, Honolulu, Hawaii

Carol is a children's book author. She came to my school and presented her book. She is very engaging and the students loved her singing and storytelling. She was very professional and brought all of the equipment that she would need. I would highly recommend her to any library. Twas the Mouse Before Christmas is a new perspective to the traditional Clement Moore poem 'Twas the Night Before Christmas. Dabney captures the essence of children's difficulty in falling asleep on Christmas Eve. Children will love this new take on an old story. Even more special is the music and words to a song written by Dabney. A true trademark of Carol Dabney's work. - Belinda Self, Media Specialist, literacy teacher Harrisburg, Arkansas

The Mouse before Christmas is a very sweet new addition to our love for Christmas stories. I do believe one day it will become a classic. The hard working dedicated mouse reminds me of the author of this book. It's very easy reading and I loved the illustrations, and children as well as adults will enjoy the mouse before Christmas, - much Aloha Arlene Hasegawa, grandmother, Hilo, Hawaii

A very intriguing, creative, delightfully different children's story which captivates the imagination with its whimsical rhyming story and beautifully illustrated caricatures. The plot, pace, and smooth blend of story and illustrations are guaranteed to keep a child's interest from start to finish. This is certainly a book any child will want to return to read over and over again. The entertainment does not stop with the story's end, for there is an easy bake cookie recipe offered for children to prepare, and, a Christmas Song (both lyrics and music) accompany the book's text and eye catching illustrations. Children can both read along and sing along — what complete entertainment can you find anywhere else. And, as a uniquely added plus, the book is offered with multi-lingual text in both English and Spanish. This book offers so much to be enjoyed. I would highly recommend it to anyone. The Arkansas Reviewer

'Twas The Mouse before Christmas is a fresh take on a timeless treasure. Christmas from the mouse's view… precious! –Phllis Jones LT. Col Buckley Air Force Base, Colorado

"Twas the Mouse Before Christmas"

This colorful Christmas story is sure to delight and Harold's gift to Santa shows the true spirit of Christmas! And it's both in English and Spanish. Feliz Navidad! Sylvia Hashimoto, singer-songwriter Keaau, Hawaii

A very cute story for all. It would be a great story to share in class to show students how you can take a classic story and add to it or make it your own. -Elena Reyes Lovins, Gifted and Talented teacher for North Little Rock School District, National Board Certified Teacher.

'Twas the mouse is a great story about love and giving. This little mouse comes alive in this wonderful children's book. Harold will make you smile as he bakes the night away making sure Santa has his cookies, from finding a recipe to taking care of the house, and all the creatures. Fun to bake the cookies and sing the song included in this very charming fun tradition to add to your Christmas from now on. Carol Dabney has written both the story and created all the art work for this wonderful book. She has added both English and Spanish, a beautiful song written by her Christmas in your Heart, and of course a cookie recipe. It is packed full of Christmas cheer and I would recommend it to everyone.   -Barbara Funk of www. FunksGallery.com   online shop at Etsy.com, Pioneer, California.

'Twas Mouse Before Christmas" is such a delightful story! It combines holiday magic and the spirit of giving that set the mood for that special night!   "El Ratoncito y la Nochebuena" es un cuento encantador. Combina el mágico navideño con un espíritu generoso y estas dos cosas establecen el ambiente para esa noche especial. -Cindy Reyes, Spanish teacher, Little Rock, Arkansas

Oh this looks awesome. So cute and warm! I love it. —Christopher Dabney, Computer Engineer, San Jose, California

A cute addition to any Christmas tradition. —Jeff Woods, of www.RedWoodsPhotography. com   Little Rock, Arkansas

"Carol is one of the most amazingly talented people I have had the pleasure to meet. Her ability writing books shows in those she has completed and those soon to come. Her art work and painting is another side of talent that continues to impress and when she sings and composes music her ability and talent shines brightly. When speaking she inspires all who have the privilege to attend."   More Than Just A Story in a Book by Linda Nance NEA Writers Group www.linda-nance.blogspot.com

Some blogs that you'll want to visit for more kid friendly reviews: asimplelifereally.blogspot.com

Made in the USA
San Bernardino, CA
29 November 2019